MW00335080

Look up into the sky. Can you see the rainbow? It arches like a bridge over the hills and comes down into Nutshell Wood. At the end of the rainbow, deep in the wood, a tiny magical village is appearing. That village is Rainbow's End. Rainbow's End can only be seen by humans when a rainbow is in the sky, otherwise it is invisible to everyone except the gnomes who live there and the woodland animals.

The gnomes of Rainbow's End are jolly little folk who are always busy. Lots of exciting and interesting things happen in the village and no one is ever bored. This book tells the story of something that happened there. A little bird told me!

Rainbow's End
The Wonderful Whatsisname
Written by Jane Patience
Illustrated by John Patience

This 1987 edition published by Derrydale Books,
Distributed by Crown Publishers Inc.,
225 Park Avenue South, New York, N. Y. 10003.
© Peter Haddock Ltd: Rainbow's End Productions.
Printed in Hungary

ISBN 0-517-64967-5

It was Spring and Woolly Foot was out in Nutshell Wood. He had been to visit his friend the owl in her home by the waterfall and they had spent a pleasant morning together, discussing this and that. As he strolled along, Woolly Foot noticed a dark area in the side of a hill. "That's funny," he thought. "I've never noticed that before. I'd better investigate." He found that it was a cave, so he went inside. After a few moments, when his eyes had got used to the poor light, Woolly Foot saw something that made him gasp with amazement.

Right in the middle of the cave was the most beautiful thing Woolly Foot had ever seen. It was a large stone but not just any old stone. This one was covered with swirling patterns in an amazing assortment of bright colours. Gnomes are very fond of precious stones and Woolly Foot was no exception, so he decided that he must get this one home somehow. It was very hard work and several times he felt like giving up, but eventually Woolly Foot reached the edge of Rainbow's End. He gave the giant stone one last shove and it began to roll down the steep hill into the village. "Look out!" he cried as it bounced down the bumpy path. Gnomes scattered in all directions and the huge stone came to rest in the middle of the village green.

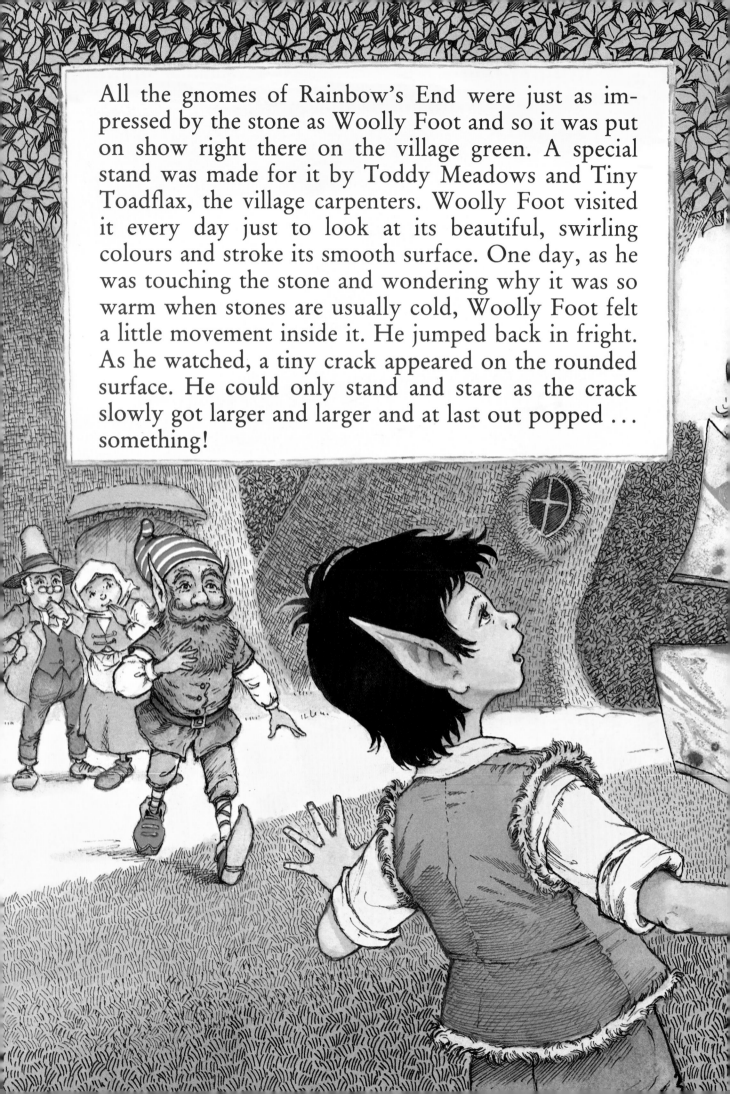

All the gnomes of Rainbow's End were just as impressed by the stone as Woolly Foot and so it was put on show right there on the village green. A special stand was made for it by Toddy Meadows and Tiny Toadflax, the village carpenters. Woolly Foot visited it every day just to look at its beautiful, swirling colours and stroke its smooth surface. One day, as he was touching the stone and wondering why it was so warm when stones are usually cold, Woolly Foot felt a little movement inside it. He jumped back in fright. As he watched, a tiny crack appeared on the rounded surface. He could only stand and stare as the crack slowly got larger and larger and at last out popped ... something!

It was a very strange something indeed. By now quite a crowd had gathered on the village green and they all agreed that they had never seen anything like this before. Obviously, the stone was really an egg, but this was no bird that had hatched out. It was a very odd looking animal. "What's his name?" asked one of the small children who were staring with wide eyes. "I don't know," Woolly Foot replied. "We'll just have

to call it 'Whatsisname'." He moved forward to stroke the creature. Like any newly-hatched chick, the Whatsisname decided that the first moving thing it saw must be its mother and so that's what Woolly Foot became. The Whatsisname followed him everywhere.

As the days passed, the Whatsisname grew at an alarming rate. Before long it was bigger than Woolly Foot and beginning to cause problems. Woolly Foot discovered that the only thing Whatsisname would eat was a herb that grew in parts of Nutshell Wood. They would spend nearly all day there so that the strange animal could satisfy its enormous appetite. And at night things were no easier; the Whatsisname insisted on sleeping on Woolly Foot's bed. This had been rather nice when it was newly-hatched, but now there was hardly room for the boy and so he took to sleeping on the floor! Whatsisname certainly did make life difficult for Woolly Foot, but he couldn't help loving the funny creature and it certainly loved him, too.

One night, when all Rainbow's End was sleeping, strange eerie sounds drifted through the village from the wood. It was like a sort of sad, moaning song, and some of the gnomes half heard it and stirred in their sleep. At the Oaksbeards' home, Woolly Foot was sound asleep, but the Whatsisname woke from its dream and sat up, straining its ears to catch the sound. The song awoke a longing in the young animal and it crept out of the house and away into the woods.

When Woolly Foot woke up in the morning and saw that the Whatsisname was gone, he was very worried. "It's too young to look after itself," he said to his mother and father. So he set off to follow the tracks the Whatsisname had made in the muddy ground. The footprints led Woolly Foot through the woods, ignoring paths and tracks, in a straight line towards the cave where he had found the egg. When he reached the cave, Woolly Foot saw that the tracks went inside, and he crept in.

This time there was no beautiful egg but something even more astonishing. Right there in the cave were the little Whatsisname and two very big Whatsisnames!

They were so enormous that Woolly Foot felt very scared. He wondered what they might do to him, but he needn't have worried. When the baby Whatsisname saw the boy it ran across and gave him a friendly lick. The mother and father Whatsisnames quickly forgave Woolly Foot for stealing their egg – after all, it was a mistake. In fact, the Whatsisname family became very friendly with the gnomes of Rainbow's End and in the summertime they all went on picnics together. The Whatsisnames were very fond of the gnome children and let them slide down their backs. They said it felt tickly!

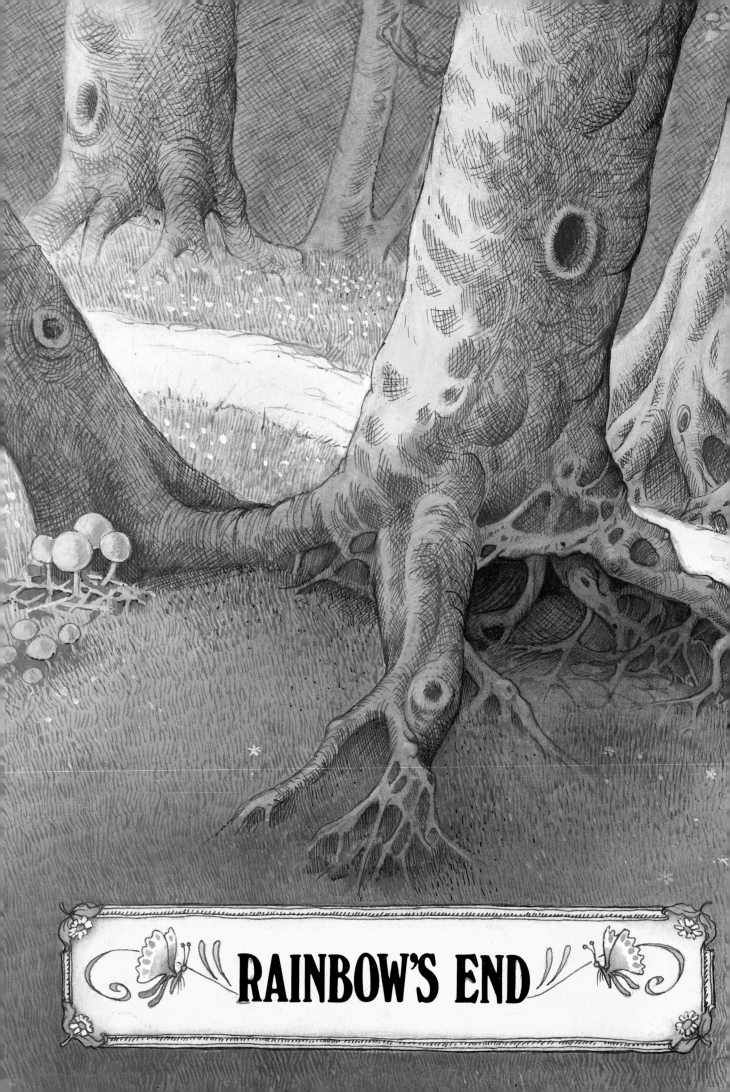

RAINBOW'S END